SHAKESPEARE FOR EVERYONE

KING LEAR

By Jennifer Mulherin and Abigail Frost
Illustrations by Gwen Green
CHERRYTREE BOOKS

Author's note

There is no substitute for seeing the plays of Shakespeare performed. Only then can you really understand why Shakespeare is our greatest dramatist and poet. This book simply gives you the background to the play and tells you about the story and characters. It will, I hope, encourage you to see the play.

A Cherrytree Book

Designed and produced by
A S Publishing

First published 1990
by Cherrytree Press Ltd
327 High Street
Slough
Berkshire SL1 1TX

Reprinted 1995, 1997, 2001

Copyright this edition © Evans Brothers Ltd 2001

British Library Cataloguing in Publication Data
Mulherin, Jennifer
 King Lear
 I. Title II. Series III Frost, Abigail.
 822.3'3

ISBN 1 84234 046 8

Printed in Hong Kong through Colorcraft Ltd

Contents

King Lear *and women of power and property*

King Lear is unusual among Shakespeare's plays in that three of the most important characters are women. Women were played by boys on the stages of Shakespeare's time, and perhaps he could not always rely on having so many in his company who were good enough actors to play major parts.

Today it does not seem strange to see women – Cordelia, Goneril and Regan – as powerful rulers, leading armies to war with ruthless confidence. We have seen women prime ministers, such as Margaret Thatcher of Britain, Golda Meir of Israel and Benazir Bhutto of Pakistan, govern coolly and firmly in times of war and civil disturbance. But to people who lived between our time and Shakespeare's, it would have seemed extraordinary. Though not, perhaps, in Shakespeare's lifetime, when many women became powerful, rich and famous.

A Virgin Queen

The most famous, rich and powerful of them all was Queen Elizabeth I. Elizabeth reigned for 45 years. She was the daughter of a magnificent Renaissance prince (as all great rulers were called then), Henry VIII, and she was determined to live up to her heritage. Cordelia, in the play, points out that her father's demand for all her love is excessive:

Bess of Hardwick. She saw three wealthy husbands to the grave, and then quarrelled with the fourth.

> *Sure, I shall never marry like my sisters*
> *To love my father all.*

Elizabeth – who certainly loved her father – would have seen the logic of this, though she had been dead three years when the play was performed. She never married, even though it was an age when baby princesses were sometimes solemnly betrothed to baby princes to serve their parents' political ends.

Elizabeth wanted to be a real 'prince' like her father, and that meant bowing her head to nobody. A wife was expected to submit to her husband – so a 'prince' could not be a wife. Instead, as she once told parliament, she thought of herself as married to her country.

4

Bess left her last husband, the Earl of Shrewsbury, and moved back home. There she transformed her father's plain manor house into one of the greatest houses in the land. Her initials, ES, were built into the roof line and decorated the walls of the best rooms.

Rich widows

For royal ladies and the daughters of the greatest lords marriage was normally a political matter. For them and for those who owned property or businesses, it was a way of building up or preserving the family fortune. When a woman married, her property or money passed to her husband. As part of the marriage contract, the wife's family would provide a dowry in the form of money or land which would pass to the husband. Lear's refusal to give Cordelia a dowry would have been seen as devastating to her.

The husband or his family were expected to provide a jointure – enough money to keep the wife if he died first. In the City of London, a merchant's widow had a right to a third of her late husband's wealth (two-thirds if they had no children), and of course he might leave her more. So a woman who saw several husbands to the grave might build up a large fortune of her own. One such was the Countess of Shrewsbury, known as 'Bess of Hardwick'.

Bess started life fairly humbly. She was the third daughter of a country squire in Derbyshire, but at 14 she married a rich, but unhealthy young man. He died soon after and left her all his money. With this, she bought Hardwick House, her family home, from her brother.

The widow married two more rich men, and had six children by one of them. She also persuaded the first to sell his own lands and buy more land in Derbyshire, near Hardwick. By 1568, she was widowed for the third time, and very rich indeed. The greatest lord in the land, George, Earl of Shrewsbury, wanted to marry her. But first, she insisted that two of her daughters should marry his sons. This ensured that his wealth would always stay in her family.

These women have gone to fetch medicine for the baby. Poisons could also be had from an unscrupulous apothecary – for a price.

A villainess of deepest dye

Bess was a tough character, but hardly a villain on the lines of Goneril and Regan. There was at least one woman of their evil kind, however, in Shakespeare's time, though he would not have known of her until after he wrote *Lear*. Frances Howard, daughter of the Earl of Suffolk, was married at 15 to the 14-year-old Earl of Essex. But she could not love this feeble boy, and soon fell for Robert Carr, another courtier. Robert's best friend, the poet Sir Thomas Overbury, helped him write letters and poems to her. But Overbury started to disapprove when Frances decided to divorce Essex.

Divorce was very difficult then, and expensive. An Archbishop had to look at the couple's story and give permission – which rarely happened. But Frances succeeded. Meanwhile, Overbury was doing what he could to stop Frances and Robert marrying. They used their influence to have him imprisoned in the Tower of London. But this was not enough for Frances.

She managed to get the Warden of the Tower to hire a cook who was in her pay. The cook poisoned Overbury's food,

These 'fishwives' are running their own business, gutting and selling fish.

6

but, though he became ill, he lived. Frances sent him sweets and tarts laced with arsenic. Overbury grew weaker and weaker, but still did not die. So Frances sent an apothecary with 'medicine' for him – poison again. This finished poor Sir Thomas off.

It was two years before anyone suspected what had happened, but in 1616 the couple (by now Earl and Countess of Suffolk) were tried before the House of Lords. The cook and apothecary were executed for murder, while the noble couple managed to get off with imprisonment.

Queens of the house

Though most women did not have such eventful lives as Elizabeth, Bess, or Frances, they were often well educated. With Elizabeth on the throne, few dared speak against education for women. Young upper-class women learnt Latin, Greek, French and Italian and were encouraged to take an interest in politics. The wives of craftsmen and farmers were often involved in the business side of their husbands' work, keeping the accounts and seeing that money owed was paid, while the husband ran his workshop or farm. All women were expected to know something about medicine (perhaps this is why Frances and Goneril were so handy with poison). The flax and egg-white dressing Cornwall's servants find for Gloucester is a typical housewife's remedy of the time.

During the reign of James I, who succeeded Elizabeth, the fashion changed. Girls were usually not taught the classics. But women of the time were far from being retiring. Later, during the Civil War (1642-46), women on both sides bravely defended their homes while their husbands were away in the army, firing cannons themselves and sometimes preferring death to surrender.

The spirit of Cordelia, and Elizabeth, lived on.

Ancient kings and wise fools

The action of *King Lear* takes place in Ancient Britain. The chronicler Geoffrey of Monmouth (who died about 1155) tells us that King Lear lived just before the founding of Rome (traditionally, 753bc) and the time when Isaiah was making his prophecies in Israel. But this does not mean that there was ever a real King Lear, though perhaps there was an early Celtic chief who divided his lands among his daughters. Though there was no writing in very early times, people loved to tell stories, and some memories might have been preserved this way.

The most famous of the legendary kings of Britain was King Arthur. There is a small amount of evidence for him being 'real'. There was a Celtic chief who tried to fight off the Saxons after the Romans left Britain. By Geoffrey's reckoning, Arthur lived 1200 years after Lear. One of the Fool's jokes mentions his wizard, Merlin. The Fool speaks a nonsense 'prophecy', and adds: 'This prophecy Merlin shall make, for I live before his time'.

The Fool

There were several versions of the story of King Lear before Shakespeare's, but none of them mentions the Fool. Shakespeare must have invented him as a way of showing up Lear's own folly. Tudor kings and queens had court fools – or jesters – to amuse them. Fools could also tell their masters things (about their faults, or about scandals at court) that others might be executed for saying, because they did it in a way that sounded like a joke. Henry VIII's fool, Will Somers, was said to be one of the closest people to him. Perhaps

Edgar slipped easily into the guise of Poor Tom. One more 'Bedlam beggar' would not be noticed in a time when the poor had to rely on charity from the rich. When Lear is cast out into the storm, he understands for the first time the plight of these 'poor naked wretches'. He says: 'O! I have ta'en too little care of this.'

Henry, always trying to get rid of one wife and take another, needed someone who was not involved in politics to talk to.

There were many kinds of fool. Some, sadly, were deformed or handicapped people whose only way of making a living was to let people laugh at their 'funny' way of moving or talking, and hope they would throw them pennies. It was a cruel age in some ways. But by Shakespeare's time there were professional fools, talented comedians, dancers or tumblers who had chosen that way of life and put a lot of work and thought into their own special acts. They were the comedy stars of their time. Some of them, of course, worked for Shakespeare's theatre company.

Will Kempe was one. He was an old-fashioned type of fool, who danced jigs, sang comic songs and told his own jokes

Left: Velasquez's painting, the Idiot of Coria. *Dwarfs and handicapped people often earned their living by becoming fools.*

Right: The fool, Thomas Kempe, danced a jig from London to Norwich. He wrote a book about it, called Kempe's Nine Days' Wonder.

Below: Robert Armin played the Fool in King Lear. He also wrote books and a play for children.

on stage, whether they were relevant to Shakespeare's story or not. Eventually, the company sacked him. (Perhaps Shakespeare was fed up with the man changing his lines.)

Kempe was not deterred; he decided to make money by dancing a jig from London to Norwich, collecting money on the way.

His replacement was Robert Armin, who played the Fool in *King Lear*. Armin's style of comedy was subtler, relying more on word-play than falling about or repeating tired catch-phrases. He must also have had a good singing voice; Shakespeare wrote many beautiful, sad songs for him. He was obviously a thoughtful man; like Kempe, he was also an author, but he loved to write about the history of fools in general, rather than simply puff his own exploits.

In *King Lear*, Shakespeare uses all Armin's stage talents to create a unique character, one who sings, dances, talks sense and nonsense, and is at once funny and sad.

The story of King Lear

All the lords of Britain are gathered to hear the ageing King Lear's future plans. The earls of Gloucester and Kent are speculating about what he will say. Gloucester introduces Edmund, his illegitimate son, to Kent. The bustling court falls silent as Lear enters with his daughters, Goneril, Regan and Cordelia, and the husbands of the elder two.

Lear speaks: today he will divide his kingdom amongst his daughters, and say which of Cordelia's two suitors may marry her. Each daughter will get a portion of land according to how much she loves her father.

Words of love

Goneril, the eldest, swears she loves her father 'dearer than eyesight, space and liberty'. Lear offers her a good share of his kingdom. Regan agrees with her sister – except, she says, that Goneril has not gone far enough. She too is assured of her share. Cordelia, the youngest, wonders what she can say in return.

Lear calls Cordelia to declare her love. What can she say to outshine the others? 'Nothing, my lord,' she replies. Lear, aghast, asks her to speak again. Cordelia protests that true love cannot be put into fine words.

Angrily, Lear declares that Cordelia will get nothing. The Earl of Kent interrupts, begging him to see sense. But the stubborn old king orders him to leave his kingdom.

Lear asks Cordelia's suitors if either will marry her, now she is a pauper, not a princess. The Duke of Burgundy refuses; but the King of France gladly offers his hand to her. Cordelia says a tearful goodbye to her sisters, who treat her scornfully. When she has gone, they reveal their true feelings: they think their father is a fool, and neither will put

Cordelia's love
> Good my lord,
> You have begot me, bred
>   me, lov'd me: I
> Return those duties back as
>   are right fit,
> Obey you, love you, and
>   most honour you.
> Why have my sisters
>   husbands, if they say
> They love you all? Haply,
>   when I shall wed,
> That lord whose hand must
>   take my plight shall
>   carry
> Half my love with him, half
>   my care and duty:
> Sure I shall never marry
>   like my sisters,
> To love my father all.
>   Act I Sc i

up with his changeable moods for long. Neither looks forward to his plan of staying alternate months with them.

A wicked son

Edmund, too, plans to deceive his father. He is resentful because, as a younger son and illegitimate, he will not inherit Gloucester's land. He has a plan to turn Gloucester against his legitimate brother, Edgar.

The old earl comes in, muttering about the strange events at court. Edmund hastily stuffs a letter into his pocket. Gloucester asks to see it. His son appears reluctant, but hands it over. It complains that old men are tyrants, who deny their sons money and power until they too are too old to enjoy them, and hints at a conspiracy against Gloucester; and it is signed 'Edgar'. The horrified Gloucester does not suspect the truth, which is that Edmund has forged the letter. He blames everything on 'these late eclipses of the sun and moon'.

Edmund has no time for eclipses and astrology; he believes that people make their own fate. When he sees Edgar, he asks him what he has done to offend Gloucester. Edgar is puzzled; they have not quarrelled. Edmund advises him to run away, and make sure to carry a weapon with him.

Kent's loyalty

Lear is staying with Goneril and her husband, the Duke of Albany. Already there is friction. The old king has struck a courtier for telling off his Fool. The hundred personal knights that accompany the king are troublesome and expensive to keep. Goneril tells Oswald, her steward, to treat Lear badly, hoping to drive him away to stay with Regan.

Kent disguises himself as a poor man, and persuades Lear to hire him as a servant. He soon gains the king's favour, and a tip, by tripping up the insolent Oswald.

Disorder in the stars
These late eclipses in the sun and moon portend no good to us: though the wisdom of nature can reason it thus and thus, yet nature finds itself scourged by the sequent effects. Love cools, friendship falls off, brothers divide: in cities, mutinies; in countries, discord; in palaces, treason; and the bond cracked between son and father.

Act I Sc ii

Goneril's complaints
By day and night he wrongs me; every hour
He flashes into one gross crime or other,
That sets us all at odds; I'll not endure it:
His knights grow riotous, and himself upbraids us
On every trifle.

Act I Sc iii

The Fool

In comes Lear's Fool – the only person the old king will accept criticism from. He makes his points in jokes and riddles. Seeing Lear tipping Kent, the Fool offers the new servant his court jester's cap. He explains that Kent must be a fool to follow a fool like Lear.

'Dost thou call me fool, boy?' asks Lear. Yes, says the Fool: 'All other titles hast thou given away; that thou wast born with.'

Goneril tells Lear to dismiss fifty knights. Enraged, Lear sets off at once to stay with Regan. Goneril sends Oswald ahead, to warn her sister that he is coming.

Edmund's plot

Lear sends Kent to Regan with his side of the story. At once Regan and her husband, the Duke of Cornwall, ride to Gloucester's castle, to ask for his advice. They take Kent and Oswald with them to await their replies.

At the castle, Edmund warns Edgar, who has been hiding, to flee, not just from his father but from Cornwall, too. He pretends to believe that Edgar has made an enemy of Cornwall. Suddenly the brothers hear Gloucester arrive. Edgar runs away into the night. Edmund cuts his own arm with his sword so that he can pretend that Edgar has attacked and wounded him.

16

Edmund tells his father that Edgar was planning to kill him. Gloucester says he will bestow his lands on Edmund.

Regan, Cornwall and their party arrive. While the nobles discuss what to do about Lear, Kent and Oswald meet and quarrel bitterly. The argument turns into a fight. Cornwall intervenes and puts Kent into the stocks – a grave insult to his royal master.

Kent is secretly glad to be alone in the stocks; it gives him a chance to read a letter from Cordelia. She and the King of France have plans.

Lear dispossessed

Lear and the Fool arrive at Regan's palace, to find nobody home. They proceed to Gloucester's castle, and find Kent in the stocks. Lear is outraged at this new insult, and even more by his daughter's refusal to let him in.

Gloucester brings Regan and Cornwall out, and Kent is released. Lear greets Regan kindly, and starts to tell her how Goneril has mistreated him. She cuts him short, saying her sister was in the right and telling him to go back and beg forgiveness. Then Goneril herself arrives.

'Art not ashamed to look upon this beard?' asks Lear. Though Regan greets her sister warmly, the king still believes she will take him, hundred knights and all. As they

17

talk, however, the number of knights each will accept falls. Regan says she can take only twenty-five – so Lear says he will go with Goneril, who will let him have fifty. But Goneril says he does not need any knights at all – there are plenty of servants at her palace.

Crying for revenge, Lear walks out. A terrible storm is brewing, but his daughters do not try to stop him.

Kent and the Fool are the only followers Lear has left. Kent sends a messenger to Cordelia, who has secretly landed at Dover with the King of France's army.

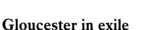

The blasted heath

Lear and his two loyal servants wander over a lonely heath. The old king shouts defiantly at the thunder and lightning; cruel as they are, they are not as bad as his ungrateful daughters. He is losing his mind. Kent gently leads his master to the shelter of a tiny hovel.

Gloucester in exile

Regan turns Gloucester out of his own home, for trying to defend the king. He complains of this to Edmund, and mentions a letter he has received, telling him of the French invasion. Deciding to join the king, he asks Edmund to deceive Cornwall about his plans. Edmund sees a path to power for himself. He will betray his father and tell Cornwall about the invasion.

A strange new friend

On the heath, Lear sends the Fool into the hovel. The Fool runs out, terrified of a 'spirit' inside. Its name is Poor Tom, he says – the country name for a madman.

But 'Poor Tom' is not what he seems; he is Edgar, in disguise. He shouts crazily about a foul fiend that is plaguing him. Lear, obsessed with his own troubles, asks if 'Tom's'

How many knights?

Gon. *Hear me, my lord. What need you five-and-twenty, ten, or five, To follow in a house, where twice so many Have a command to tend you?*

Reg. *What need one?*

Lear. *O! reason not the need; our basest beggars Are in the poorest thing superfluous: Allow not nature more than nature needs, Man's life is cheap as beast's.*

Act II Sc iv

18

Lear defies the storm

*Blow, winds, and crack
    your cheeks! rage! blow!
You cataracts and
    hurricanoes, spout
Till you have drench'd our
    steeples, drown'd the
    cocks!*

Act III Sc iii

daughters have driven him mad – what else could bring a man so low?

Gloucester arrives with a flaming torch, to take Lear and his friends to safety. He does not recognise Edgar, who pretends to mistake him for the fiend. Lear wants to go on talking to the madman, whose ravings seem to him like profound philosophy, but at last Gloucester leads them to an outhouse of his castle where they can hide.

There, Lear decides to try his daughters for treason. His followers – the Fool, Edgar and Kent – sit like a bench of magistrates. Stools take the place of the accused.

Kent is so upset by his old master's sad, crazed manner, that he begins to cry. Gloucester, who knows the old king's life is in danger, tells Kent to take Lear to Dover.

Cordelia will protect him there.

Gloucester is blinded

Inside the castle, news of the French invasion has arrived – and the hunt is on for Gloucester. Goneril, Edmund and Oswald set off to take the news to Albany.

Gloucester is soon caught. Regan and Cornwall question him harshly. When Gloucester says he cannot bear to see the treatment meted out to Lear, Cornwall cruelly crushes one of his eyes. Shocked by this barbarity, one of the servants attacks his master, but Regan kills him. Though gravely wounded, Cornwall has enough strength to put out Gloucester's other eye. The old man is led away, blood pouring down his face. The other servants, deserting their evil lord, bind Gloucester's wounds with flax and egg-white.

On the heath, Edgar (still disguised as 'Poor Tom') sees Gloucester coming. Gloucester asks the servant leading him to leave him with the madman. He offers 'Tom' money to take him to the cliffs of Dover.

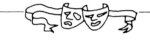

A faithless wife

Goneril and Edmund arrive at Albany's palace, to learn that he welcomes the French invasion. He hates Goneril's cruelty to her father. Goneril sends Edmund back to Regan with this news – giving him a passionate kiss. She loves the vicious Edmund far more than the husband she now despises.

Albany comes in and expresses his disgust for Goneril's attitude. A messenger brings the news that Cornwall is dead; the servant's wound proved fatal after all. Hearing how Gloucester was blinded, Albany swears to avenge him.

Summons to arms

Cordelia now knows her father's fate. Both sad and angry, she asks a doctor if his madness can be cured. First, however, she must defeat Goneril and Regan.

The two sisters are no longer friends. Regan, now a widow, means to marry Edmund, but knows Goneril loves him too. She uses Oswald in a plan to outwit her sister. At the same time, she regrets letting Gloucester live and callously proposes that Oswald 'cuts him off', if he finds him.

A leap in the dark

Gloucester himself wants to die. As they approach Dover, he asks Edgar how much further it is to the cliff-top. Edgar tells him they are nearly there; can he not hear the sea? Gloucester cannot. He is puzzled – the madman seems different. He no longer babbles about foul fiends, but talks calmly. Edgar says they have reached the edge of the cliff; it makes him dizzy to look down.

Gloucester sends 'Tom' away. Then he jumps.

Miraculous rescue?

But his fall does not kill him. A friendly stranger helps him up, exclaiming about his miraculous survival. The stranger

> **A fearful precipice**
> *How fearful*
> *And dizzy 'tis to cast one's*
> *eyes so low!*
> *The crows and choughs that*
> *wing the midway air*
> *Show scarce so gross as*
> *beetles; half way down*
> *Hangs one that gathers*
> *samphire, dreadful*
> *trade!*
> *Methinks he seems no bigger*
> *than his head.*
> *The fishermen that walk*
> *upon the beach*
> *Appear like mice, and yond*
> *tall anchoring bark*
> *Diminish'd to her cock, her*
> *cock a buoy*
> *Almost too small for sight.*
> Act IV Sc vi

asks who it was that he saw with Gloucester on the cliff-top. 'A poor unfortunate beggar,' answers the old man. The stranger says it looked to him like a demon with horns. The gods have saved the old man from hell. Gloucester remembers how 'Poor Tom' talked of devils and fiends. He resolves to bear his troubles in future.

But the stranger is really Edgar. He led his father to the top of a little knoll, pretending it was the cliff, and cleverly prevented him from taking his own life.

Mad Lear

As they talk, Lear comes by, raving. Gloucester knows his voice and kneels to kiss his hand. Lear mistakes him for the blind god of love, Cupid. He shouts about the world's wickedness and lustfulness.

At last Lear recognises Gloucester. In his ravings, he talks of killing his enemies. Then a group of men appear, saying they have come from his 'most dear daughter'. Thinking they are from Goneril or Regan, he runs away, and they chase after him. It was Cordelia who sent them, as Gloucester and Edgar realise.

As the pair set off towards Cordelia's camp, Oswald enters. He draws his sword, but Edgar fights and kills him. As he dies, Oswald orders Edgar – not knowing who he is – to give a letter he has from Goneril to Edmund. The letter asks Edmund to kill Albany.

Lear and Cordelia reunited

At the camp, Lear is now safely asleep. Cordelia goes to see him and wakes him with a kiss. At first Lear does not believe it is her; he is overjoyed when he does.

The armies meet

Edmund and Regan are beginning to quarrel. Just as she is accusing him of loving Goneril, Goneril and Albany appear. Albany, fearing to lose his power, says that they must all fight together against the French. Edgar, still disguised, slips in and speaks to Albany while the others walk ahead. He gives the earl the letter he took from Oswald, but before Albany has time to read it, Edmund returns to say that the French army is in sight. The battle-hour has come.

A fatal letter

The British army defeats the French; Lear and Cordelia are captured. Cordelia asks to see her sisters, but Lear is happy to go straight to prison with her. Edmund sends them off to his castle, giving a letter to the captain of their guard.

Albany has now read Oswald's letter. He arrests Edmund as a traitor, and challenges him to fight one of his knights. Regan collapses. Goneril is not surprised, because she has poisoned her sister.

Reunion

I fear I am not in my perfect mind.
Methinks I should know you and know this man;
Yet I am doubtful: for I am mainly ignorant
What place this is, and all the skill I have
Remembers not these garments; nor I know not
Where I did lodge last night. Do not laugh at me;
For, as I am a man, I think this lady
To be my child Cordelia.

Act IV Sc vii

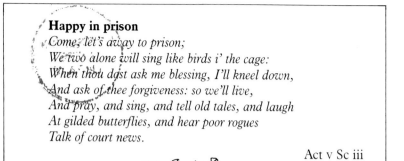

Happy in prison
Come, let's away to prison;
We two alone will sing like birds i' the cage:
When thou dost ask me blessing, I'll kneel down,
And ask of thee forgiveness: so we'll live,
And pray, and sing, and tell old tales, and laugh
At gilded butterflies, and hear poor rogues
Talk of court news.

Act v Sc iii

Edgar, in another guise, volunteers to fight against Edmund, and beats him in combat. Goneril rushes to his aid, but runs away when Albany threatens to reveal the letter's contents. As Edmund grows weaker, Edgar admits his true identity. He is now Earl of Gloucester – his father has died of grief at the news that Lear is captured.

The news comes that Regan has died of the poison and Goneril has killed herself. Edmund, with his dying breath, sends Edgar to the castle – to stop the death-warrant he sent for Lear and Cordelia.

But Cordelia has already been executed, and Lear is crazed with grief. He killed her hangman, but could not save her. He dies weeping over her body.

Cordelia's death
No, no, no life!
Why should a dog, a horse,
a rat, have life,
And thou no breath at all?
Thou'lt come no more,
Never, never, never, never,
never!
Pray you, undo this button:
thank you, sir.
Do you see this? Look on
her, look, her lips,
Look there, look there!

Act v Sc iii

Lear's grief
Howl, howl, howl, howl! O! you are men of stones:
Had I your tongues and eyes, I'd use them so
That heaven's vaults should crack. She's gone for ever.
I know when one is dead, and when one lives;
She's dead as earth. Lend me a looking-glass; If that her
breath will mist or stain the stone,
Why, then she lives.

Act v Sc iii

The play's characters

Lear

Lear

The old king's trouble is that he wants the advantages of power even when he has given it up. He expects to be treated like a king even when he has nothing. But he learns from his terrible experiences. While once he required a hundred knights to hold his head up, by the end of the play he realises that all he needs in the world is Cordelia's love. He has lived with 'poor naked wretches', and thought, in his madness, about the falseness of human power and justice. He has learnt the hard way that those who speak the finest words, like Regan and Goneril, do not always have the finest feelings.

Cordelia

Lear's youngest daughter is truthful to a fault. She cannot flatter her father as her sisters do, and so loses her share of the kingdom. But the King of France realises that she is really the best of the three, and is happy to marry her. She is a

Cordelia

courageous queen, able to lead an invading army to her father's rescue. When she discovers the full and sad truth about what has happened to Lear, she is appalled; she would treat even a dog better than that. Against Lear's rants about the basic cruelty of humans, we must place her sense of charity.

Cordelia's kindness

Mine enemy's dog,
Though he had bit me,
should have stood that
night
Against my fire. And wast
though fain, poor father,
To hovel thee with swine
and rogues forlorn,
In short and musty straw!
Alack, alack!

Act IV Sc vii

The sisters assess their father

Gon. *You see how full of changes his age is; the observation we have made of it hath not been little: he always loved our sister most; and with what poor judgment he hath now cast her off appears too grossly.*
Reg. *'Tis the infirmity of his age; yet he hath ever but slenderly known himself.*

Act I Sc i

Regan

Goneril

Albany's contempt

Tigers, not daughters, what have you perform'd?
A father, and a gracious aged man,
Whose reverence the head-lugg'd bear would lick,
Most barbarous, most degenerate!

Act IV Sc ii

Regan

Regan seems less cruel to Lear at first – he goes to her when life at Goneril's court becomes impossible, thinking she will let him live as he wants. But she turns out as bad as her sister. She is physically even crueller, being willing to finish the blinding of Gloucester when the servants attack Cornwall.

Kent

The Earl of Kent is a fiery, quarrelsome spirit. Like Edgar, he enjoys the chance to show his inner self through disguise. His loyalty to Lear and Cordelia survives even banishment, and he is a vital link between the two when Cordelia is in France.

Goneril

Lear's eldest daughter is cruel and vicious. She cannot bear being married to a good man like Albany, but prefers Edmund, as wicked as herself. Even when Lear is first living with her, she lets her servants ill-treat his beloved Fool. She has no loyalties at all, even poisoning her own sister when she becomes a rival for Edmund's love.

Kent

Kent insults the villainous Oswald

A knave, a rascal, an eater of broken meats; a base, proud, shallow,
beggarly, three-suited, hundred-pound, filthy, worsted-stocking knave;
a lily-liver'd, action-taking knave; a whoreson, glass-gazing,
superserviceable, finical rogue; one-trunk-inheriting slave; one that
wouldst be a bawd, in way of good service, and art nothing but the
composition of a knave, beggar, coward, pandar, and the son and heir
of a mongrel bitch: one whom I will beat into clamorous whining if thou
deniest the least syllable of thy addition.

Act II Sc ii

The Fool

The Fool may be the wisest person in the play. A poor boy who lives by his wits (and his wit), he cannot afford the pride shown by his betters, such as Lear and Cordelia. His way of looking at the world is strangely twisted, but he sees how foolish Lear has been (and tells him so) before anyone else.

Gloucester

Fool

The Fool's song

He that has a little tiny wit,
*   With hey, ho, the wind*
*   and the rain,*
Must make content with his
*   fortunes fit,*
*   Though the rain it*
*   raineth every day.*
                    Act III Sc ii

Gloucester

My duty cannot suffer
To obey in all your
*   daughters' hard*
*   commands:*
                    Act III Sc iv

Gloucester, like Lear, is too easily taken in by flattery. He listens too readily to Edmund's lies about his brother, but when his character is tested he proves loyal and even brave, defying Cornwall and Regan even while they torture him.

Edmund

Thou, Nature, art my
*   goddess; to thy law*
My services are bound.
                    Act I Sc ii

Edmund is a stage villain who knows no loyalty except to himself, but he has a tiny spark of goodness in him, which shows when he tries to save Lear and Cordelia from execution as he dies.

Edgar

Edgar is a strange character. He is not quite all good, just as Edmund is not quite all bad; he is touchy, and a little devious. He obviously enjoys playing the madman, 'Poor Tom', and the chance this 'part' gives him to complain about the wicked ways of the world. He shows great sensitivity when he lets his blind father believe that he has been saved from death by a miracle. He is deeply moved by Lear's plight.

Edg. [Aside.] *My tears*
begin to take his part so
*   much,*
They'll mar my
*   counterfeiting.*   Act III Sc vi

Edgar

Edmund

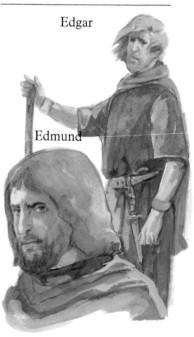

The life and plays of Shakespeare

Life of Shakespeare

1564 William Shakespeare born at Stratford-upon-Avon.

1582 Shakespeare marries Anne Hathaway, eight years his senior.

1583 Shakespeare's daughter, Susanna, is born.

1585 The twins, Hamnet and Judith, are born.

1587 Shakespeare goes to London.

1591-2 Shakespeare writes *The Comedy of Errors*. He is becoming well-known as an actor and writer.

1592 Theatres closed because of plague.

1593-4 Shakespeare writes *Titus Andronicus* and *The Taming of the Shrew*: he is member of the theatrical company, the Chamberlain's Men.

1594-5 Shakespeare writes *Romeo and Juliet*.

1595 Shakespeare writes *A Midsummer Night's Dream*.

1595-6 Shakespeare writes *Richard II*.

1596 Shakespeare's son, Hamnet, dies. He writes *King John* and *The Merchant of Venice*.

1597 Shakespeare buys New Place in Stratford.

1597-8 Shakespeare writes *Henry IV*.

1599 Shakespeare's theatre company opens the Globe Theatre.

1599-1600 Shakespeare writes *As You Like It*, *Henry V* and *Twelfth Night*.

1600-01 Shakespeare writes *Hamlet*.

1602-03 Shakespeare writes *All's Well That Ends Well*.

1603 Elizabeth I dies. James I becomes king. Theatres closed because of plague.

1603-04 Shakespeare writes *Othello*.

1605 Theatres closed because of plague.

1605-06 Shakespeare writes *Macbeth* and *King Lear*.

1606-07 Shakespeare writes *Antony and Cleopatra*.

1607 Susanna Shakespeare marries Dr John Hall. Theatres closed because of plague.

1608 Shakespeare's granddaughter, Elizabeth Hall, is born.

1609 *Sonnets* published. Theatres closed because of plague.

1610 Theatres closed because of plague. Shakespeare gives up his London lodgings and retires to Stratford.

1611-12 Shakespeare writes *The Tempest*.

1613 Globe Theatre burns to the ground during a performance of Henry VIII.

1616 Shakespeare dies on 23 April.

Shakespeare's plays

The Comedy of Errors
Love's Labour's Lost
Henry VI Part 2
Henry VI Part 3
Henry VI Part 1
Richard III
Titus Andronicus
The Taming of the Shrew
The Two Gentlemen of Verona
Romeo and Juliet
Richard II
A Midsummer Night's Dream
King John
The Merchant of Venice
Henry IV Part 1
Henry IV Part 2
Much Ado About Nothing
Henry V
Julius Caesar
As You Like It
Twelfth Night
Hamlet
The Merry Wives of Windsor
Troilus and Cressida
All's Well That Ends Well
Othello
Measure for Measure
King Lear
Macbeth
Antony and Cleopatra
Timon of Athens
Coriolanus
Pericles
Cymbeline
The Winter's Tale
The Tempest
Henry VIII

Index

Numerals in *italics* refer to picture captions.

Acknowledgements
The publishers would like to thank Patrick Rudd and Tom Deas for their help in producing this book.

Picture credits
p.1 Governors of Royal Shakespeare Theatre, p.3 private collection (photo Bridgeman Art Library), p.4 National Trust, Photographic Library/Angelo Hornak, p.5 National Trust Photographic Library/Mike Williams, p.10 Prado, Madrid (photo Bridgeman Art Library).